The Flock Unseen

four stories

A.S. Coomer

Clare Songbirds Publishing House Book Series
ISBN 978-1-947653-71-9
Clare Songbirds Publishing House
The Flock Unseen © 2019 A.S. Coomer

Printed in the United States of America
FIRST EDITION

Clare Songbirds Publishing House Mission Statement:
Clare Songbirds Publishing House was established to provide a print forum for the creation of limited edition, fine art from poets and writers, both established and emerging. We strive to reignite and continue a tradition of quality, accessible literary arts to the national and international community of writers, and readers. Manuscripts are carefully chosen for their ability to propel the expansion of art and ideas in literary form. We provide an accessible way to promote the art of words in order to resonate with, and impact, readers not yet familiar with the siren song of poets and writers. Clare Songbirds Publishing House espouses a singular cultural development where poetry creates community and becomes commonplace in public places.

140 Cottage Street
Auburn, New York 13021
www.claresongbirdspub.com

Contents

Acknowledgments:

The Flock Unseen was first published by the Merida Review.

Polly Jean was first published by Oxford Magazine.

Attempts. Failures. was first published by GFT Press.

A Truly Ugly River was first published by Flash Fiction Magazine.

For all the hearts aflutter & all the painbirds that linger.
For every beating of clipped wing & bruised heart.
May you find & may you shine a little light.
~A.S. Coomer

The Flock Unseen

The sirens woke me. I opened my eyes to the flashing red lights coming in through the closed blinds. My first conscious breath was painful, something spiked and bristled in my chest and I couldn't complete it. I sputtered and coughed and tried to swing my feet over the side of the bed to sit up but couldn't.

"Don't."

I looked over and my wife was standing there. Deep pockets of weary concern on her face.

How many times had this moment occurred?

Too many.

"They just got here," she said, placing a cold hand on my shoulder. "Don't move. Sit still."

I tried to let myself fall back onto the bed but anything other than holding myself completely rigid sent the painbirds fluttering. They're finicky creatures.

"Lie still."

From somewhere below and off to the left, the front door opened. I didn't hear it, but I felt the change in the house's pressure. It was new enough, still not really settled, that you could feel things like that.

She had her arms wrapped around herself now. Her frail hands, an old woman's hands I could see now, were stroking her naked arms. Consoling herself. The hands and slight enfolding embrace an attempt to tell herself it was going to be ok.

I tried to find her eyes.

I opened my mouth to call her name.

Nothing came out.

Two women came through the bedroom door, official and stone-faced. I thought I recognized one of them from another time, another lesser visit.

There was a fresh fluttering of the wings in my chest and I couldn't help but close my eyes. Tears snuck past the corners of my closed eyelids and streaked down both of my hot, fevered cheeks; icy slalom skiers making one last run.

When I could open my eyes again, she was talking to them. She had stepped further away from the bed, back against the wall, another enclosure giving her a sense of herself alone, confined and self-contained, her lips moving and eyes bright with anxiety, with uselessness, with time.

I tried to say her name again but couldn't. A soft avian chitter in the night followed by the flock unseen's full response. The birds were really singing now.

They came and threw back the sheets. I felt a wave of chill thrill across my wasted legs, my half-exposed stomach poking out from under the ruffled pajama shirt, the folds of my weather-beaten neck pulling back a bit, just a fraction tighter.

The understanding that the cold slowly sucked you back in time dawned on me like the first glimpse of clear-skied December sunrise. Seconds began to flash back-wards, abandoning their forward march as if it had all just been another training exercise, a fire drill, a cursory, fretless, feckless thing.

I tried to look toward my wife, but my eyes were not the eyes I closed the late April night before. They were not even the eyes of my seventy-sixth year.

I saw her through eyes ten years younger, misting around the edges; all slightly out of focus but in a very nice Coppola sort of way. She was smiling in earnest—not realizing I was watching—at the rising Minnesotan sun, her first poured cup of sugary black coffee steaming up in swirls around her chin, giving her the appearance of some beautifully aged, asiatic sage.

"What is it?"

I must've blinked because then I saw her through eyes at least twenty-five years younger, sepia-toned and warmly hazy. She was coming in through the door of the old house we used to live in downtown, her arms laden with plastic grocery bags, her face flushed from the summer heat. Little hairs were stuck to her forehead and her dark hair looked frizzled and wild. Her smooth face was florid but content. She unloaded herself onto the kitchen table and wiped her forehead with her forearm then saw me. The smile streaked across her face like heat lightning, late evenings in early August.

My stomach dropped. The birds sang louder.

I saw her, again, through eyes I've had at least fifty years since. She was sitting across from me in a little booth for two at a Mexican restaurant somewhere in the flaxen wastes of Kansas, ballcap on her head, tinted lip balm colored in slightly outside the lines of her mouth, beautiful and famished after a long day in the car. Her large eyes, anchored wonderfully in her smooth, sun kissed cheeks, were scanning the sticky, plastic shrouded menu. I watched them bloom as they lighted on what she wanted.

"Ma'am, I need you to step back."

"What's happening."

"Ma'am."

"Do something."

The birds sang another note, it surrounded me, and I felt the feathers ruffle against my chest. I opened my eyes, but everything was dark. They nestled closer and I, too, began to sing.

Polly Jean

The sun, like embers in a rekindled fire, burned through the budding dogwood blooms. Polly Jean was nestled with her tattered blankets, her breath puffing from her nostrils in thin, white tendrils in the early morning chill.

"Honey," Richard said, nudging Polly Jean. "Honey, wake up."

She moved away from his touch, pulled the covers over her head.

"Polly Jean," he shook the place under the covers where he thought her shoulders were, "we gotta get to moving."

She moaned but came to waking.

"Feels like I just went to sleep," she complained.

"The suns up," Richard said. "We got to be moving on."

She stretched, rubbed the crust from her eyes, then came out from beneath the covers. The sun, as if waiting for just that moment, broke through the foliage and lit her face with what could've passed as golden early spring light.

"God, you're beautiful," Richard whispered.

Polly Jean jerked her head towards him and narrowed her eyes into slits.

Richard's face flushed and he shot to his feet and began brushing the grass and bits of earth from his thin, worn jeans.

"I slept like a rock," he said.

He turned and scanned the copse of dogwood while Polly Jean rose, stretched, and folded her blankets.

"Let's go," Polly Jean said.

-

Nothing stirred. They came out onto the highway and not a car or truck was to be found. They walked south, the direction they'd been heading—together—for the past three days.

He was looking at her.

"What?" Polly Jean asked.

For the second time that morning, Richard's face reddened.

"Nothing," he mumbled.

They walked on in silence for some time.

"They'll probably die now, you know," he said.

"What?"

"The dogwoods. It's nearly fall but that cold snap tricked them into blooming when it warmed back up. Like it was spring."

The sun moved up and the day progressed.

-

The truck barreled by without so much as a tap of the breaks. The trees around the highway flittered like ragged rooming house drapes then lapsed back into stillness. Polly Jean let her arm drop to her side and sighed.

"Asshole," Richard said.

They walked on. The silence stretched out until it was something nearly tangible.

The road crossed a small, green river. Polly Jean stopped in the middle of the bridge and looked down. The water lazed by, slow but steady, an overfed snake making its way home.

"Let's take a minute," she said, not looking up from the water.

Richard nodded his head and waited.

-

Polly Jean found an animal's path from the bridge to the river. Richard followed her down.

She stripped in silence, setting her clothes in a neat pile on top of her pack. The bank was muddy and Polly Jean moved slowly, carefully down the gentle slope until she was waist-deep in the hunter green water. Then she dove in.

She resurfaced some fifteen yards away, near the center of the stream. She rubbed her eyes, ran her fingers through her thick and knotted hair.

She wondered how long it'd been since her last real bath. She vaguely remembered a truckstop shower somewhere in Wisconsin—after a date.

Richard was naked and shivering. He toed the water and shook more violently.

"Pussy-footing ain't gonna help you out here," she said.

He had both hands cupped around his privates.

"God but it's cold," he said.

His teeth clapped together with that last word then he broke out in a sprint into the river. He let out a battle cry and water splashed around him in a cascade of white. He tripped and flopped down, doing his best to turn his misstep into a dive.

He came up panting and red-faced.

"You are the picture of grace, Richard."

They laughed.

-

They caught a ride in the back of a rusted pickup later that afternoon. The sun was dipping behind the rolling hills, creating little pinpricks through the loblolly that fluttered like moth wings as the truck barreled south.

Richard grinned boyishly at Polly Jean, his shaggy hair whipping against his forehead. She returned the smile but something dropped in her stomach and the smile did not touch her eyes.

The man let them off somewhere on the other side of Tupelo and drove off into the burgeoning night.

"Better find a place," Richard said.

Polly Jean nodded and followed him into the thin strand of woods. The grass crinkled under their steps, already dried out from the sun, and a warm breeze ruffled the branches overhead. Everything would be auburn and gold before too long. *Shivers in sleep and frost fast on the deep sheets.*

"What?" Richard asked.

"Nothing," Polly Jean said.

They came to a gathering of thick evergreens. An eighteen-wheeler rumbled past on the highway but the sound was muted and distant.

"How about here?"

"Sure."

Polly Jean sat down her pack and started scooping handfuls of dried pine needles into a pile. She felt Richard's eyes on her but did not acknowledge him.

"If this isn't nice, I don't know what is," he said.

Polly Jean reached under the tree and raked out more needles.

The sun had long since disappeared from sight, but the night held hard to dusk and the light was plenty. She watched him step closer but still chose to ignore him.

Polly Jean unfolded her blankets and spread them out on top of the pine needles and kneaded them into the shape of a small bed.

"Polly Jean—" Richard started.

"I'll be back," she said, leaping to her feet.

She darted off into the thicket leaving Richard standing over her pallet.

Polly Jean strode into the darkening woods sweating despite the falling temperatures. She came to a stop and leaned her back against the trunk of a buck-scarred oak.

Time to move on, she kept thinking. *Time to move on. The night is long and cold and it'd been nice to share it with somebody, sure. You gotta take love where you find it.*

Love?

That's the wrong word. Comfort is more like it. You gotta take comfort where you find it. But it's time to move on.

She pushed herself off the tree and headed back to her blankets.

Richard had doubled the bed, combining his blankets with hers and plushing both with armfuls of pine needles. He was sitting with his knees pulled up to his chest, chewing on a bit of jerky.

Polly Jean looked down at him, briefly, before kneeling onto her blankets.

"Richard," she said.

He looked up from the jerky and the first bit of moonlight caught his inky eyes. They glittered in the dark, large and doe-like and she faltered.

"Let's sleep," she said.

She waited. Listening to his breathing until it came in slow, long pulls like settling water. She carefully removed his arm from her stomach and set it on his blanket. She rolled over onto her side then rose to her knees and slid out into the dew-covered ground.

She quietly folded her blankets and rolled them into her pack.

Richard sighed somewhere from within his dreams but did not stir.

Polly Jean left him sleeping in the pines. She found the road and started walking.

-

Time to move on, she repeated. Her mantra. She'd been moving since she was born and wasn't about to stop or slow down now.

A clean break is always best.

A set of headlights crested the hill behind her then settled onto the road ahead. Polly Jean turned and stared into the twin growing orbs. She stuck out her arm and projected her thumb.

The truck passed but its brake lights shone red in the darkness. It slowed to a stop, the tires rumbling on the sleeper lines sounded heavy in the stillness of the night. Muttering monsters, nighttime apparitions, making their way home.

Polly Jean trotted the fifty yards or so to the truck and peered into the passenger window. There were three men inside. The driver nodded his head to the bed. Polly Jean tossed her pack in then climbed in behind it.

The pickup jerked back onto the road. The back window slid open and the stale scent of hand-rolled cigarettes and pot wafted out.

"Hiya," the man in the middle called out.

"Hi," Polly Jean said.

"Where ya heading?"

"South."

"Want a beer?"

"Sure."

The man's heavily veined hand extended from the cab and Polly Jean took the can of Bud Light. It was warm and skunked but she drained it in deep, tear inducing pulls.

She burped into the night and crushed the can.

"Thanks," she said.

"Hot damn," the man said. "Hot damn."

They drove on late into the night. The middle passenger passed Polly Jean beer after beer and prattled on about his life. She didn't even half listen or pretend to. She sat with her back to the cab, her hair dancing in the wind and watched the road, and everything it'd held, recede.

Near to morning, the truck braked and pulled onto the shoulder. The wind raged in her ears despite being stopped; it was much like feeling the motion of the waves after a time spent in the ocean. In the red light of the brakes, a teetering man emerged looking every bit the ragged Orpheus returning haggard and alone from the underworld. He climbed slowly into the bed and sat down beside Polly Jean.

His breath came in ragged gulps and wheezes.

"Evening," he said.

Polly Jean nodded her head and sipped from the beer.

The truck started back and the wind whistled then roared and drowned out the middle passenger's ramblings.

Time to move on, she repeated. It'd taken on a

musical lilt with the buzzing of the beer in her head. *Time to move on.*

She crushed the can and let it float onto the bed with the others.

The sky was changing, a great boiling starting. To her left the deep blue was melting into a lighter hue. It was subtle but Polly Jean felt she could almost catch it if she squinted real hard.

She swayed with the truck as it navigated the pothole ridden road. She wondered vaguely if the driver was drunk.

The sky was quickening into morning. She'd missed it somehow.

They came to a halt and the driver said, "Last stop."

Polly Jean scooped up her pack and climbed out on unsteady legs.

How many beers?

"Last stop," the driver called through the window again.

The old man hadn't moved. He was slumped over with his head in the crook of his arm.

Polly Jean leaned in and shook the man's shoulder. His head lolled limply, his face coming out into the fresh morning light. The man's mouth and eyes hung open. His face was of a very pale blue.

Polly Jean gasped and jumped away from the truck and the dead man. Her legs, unsteady with the alcohol, betrayed her and she crashed onto the seat of her pants on the shoulder of the road. The motion was too much, her head felt heavier than the rest of her, and she couldn't stop herself from dropping flat on her back.

The lithe wisps of morning clouds were jarring in

their tracts. They moved left smoothly than jerked suddenly back to their starting points as if on strings or a spring of some sort. Polly Jean clamped her eyes shut and saw the man's unseeing eyes. She opened her eyes to the clouds, unnerved and sick. She rolled onto her side and threw up.

-

When she could stand, Polly Jean found the three men gathered around the passenger side of the bed staring in.

"Shit," the middle passenger said.

"Goddamn," the driver said.

The passenger reached over and clapped his hands together near the dead man's head. Once, twice, three times the passenger slapped his hands together. The dead man in the back of the truck did not move.

"Dead as a fucking doornail," the man said.

The driver spit a wad of snuff onto the shoulder. A bit of brown splashed onto Polly Jean's dirty sneakers.

Her head buzzed and spun. She took hold of the tailgate to steady herself and saw the man in the bed and the men surrounding him. She retched then retched again.

"Jesus, lady," the driver said.

"Well, we cain't call the police," the passenger said.

"Why not?" the middle passenger asked.

"I got warrants."

There was a silence between them. The road was empty, surrounded by thick woods on both sides. Somewhere near a woodpecker hammered away.

Polly Jean was sick again. She set her sweating forehead onto the lip of the tailgate and panted. Her eyes were squeezed shut and she breathed through her mouth in quick sips but still smelled the stale beer at her feet.

"What d'you want to do then?"

"I ain't catching no body. Especially not some old hobo."

Polly Jean picked her pack up and slung it over her shoulder with as little movement as she could. She straightened then started walking south, past the men and the truck.

"Hey."

"Hey, lady. Where you going?"

"Lady."

Polly Jean kept walking, training her eyes on the white line at her feet and doing her best to follow it in as straight a course as she could.

Richard flew into her mind as their calls faded. Richard had held her close. Called her "honey." Richard had smiled at her and thought her beautiful.

Time to move on.

Richard had kissed her softly. Made love to her. He wasn't just some date. A meal. A shower. A place to sleep. Richard wasn't just a fuck. He made her laugh.

Polly Jean turned and saw that she'd rounded a corner some time back and the truck was no longer visible.

Richard.

A clean break.

She crossed the median, tripping and nearly falling twice, climbed up onto the northbound lanes then on to the woods opposite. She went from tree to tree, steadying herself, watching the road when everything stopped spinning enough to turn her head. She was well out of view, hidden by the summer-thick leaves.

Her breathing was heavy in the silence, loud in her own ears. She felt sick but refused to puke again.

She walked north until the sun was well past midday. Cars and trucks had passed going in both directions. She'd expected police sirens and blue lights, but none had come.

What would she tell them if they did come and found her hiding in the woods?

They have nothing linking me back to that worn out Orpheus. I've done no wrong.

Polly Jean couldn't shake the feeling of guilt though. It permeated from her skin like a radiation sickness. It was more than the beer. More than the days without bathing. More than nights sleeping without a roof. More than the unnamed truckers and joyless acts. More than the constant shuffling of feet and blurring of landscape. It was the night without end.

Polly Jean stepped onto the shoulder of the northbound lane from the woods and stuck out her thumb.

-

"Richard," she called. "Richard."

There was no answer.

This was the spot.

She was sure of it.

"Richard."

She had walked through the woods, the end of the workday traffic a bug's hum and buzz, until she found the gentle mound of pine needles. What was to be their double bed.

Richard was gone, long gone.

Time to move on. A clean break.

Polly Jean sat down and cried.

Attempts. Failures.

There are days. And there are *these* days. The ones that stretch out before and behind you like prison sentences. Worse, death sentences.

You wake up. You go to work. You come home. You go to bed.

Repeat.

Is this life? Is this the sum total of my existence?

-

He looked back at the words the next morning, working towards the middle of his first pot of coffee.

They still meant the same thing.

"Well, that's something."

He flipped the page and started scribbling.

-

Where are the great flashes? Where are the bright excursions into understanding? Truth?

This is another day. Just like yesterday. And the day before. Just like tomorrow. Ad infinitum.

-

He sat back and drained the last of the coffee.

"Time for work."

The walk to the coffee shop wasn't exceedingly long. Detroit Avenue ran along the larger, more congested Anthony Wayne Trail and was quieter and less iffy along this stretch. The sidewalk was a challenge though. It was lifted nearly six inches in places from the intense winter freezes. He had to constantly watch his feet and where he placed them like it was a really involved, intricate dance. Something halting and oddly formal. Russian, perhaps.

He was thinking about his own intense naval gazing.

"I'm not above it. Hell, I'm probably somewhere miles below it."

Nothing and nothing and all that. It rattled around in his head like a marble, winding down and down a sewer pipe.

He knew what he wrote wasn't exceptional. It wasn't ground breaking. He wasn't the next Ernest Hemingway. He wasn't the next Flannery O'Connor. But the words had to come. They had to be scribbled out. Etched black things, crazily slanted when he was drinking or crazed in his isolation, that had to be birthed. They had to come screaming out into existence.

"They're not for anything."

They weren't. These weren't letters. They weren't intended for anyone or anything in particular. They just were.

He nodded.

There's a deep philosophical truth in that, he thought.

"They just are."

He nodded again and carefully navigated around the gnarled footroots of a towering elm.

-

Tell me anything. Tell me anything. Show me something.

-

He let the little notebook flutter shut and drop to the floor. His head buzzed like a hive of waking fire ants.

Even the coffee tasted metallic this morning. He didn't remember getting home the night before. He'd walked across the highway to the little liquor store after his shift and bought a pint of Jim Beam. He'd taken it out of the brown bag, which he used as a tissue and blew his nose, and set about pacing the railroad tracks. They crisscrossed the city like scars. They were everywhere. So prevalent they were easily forgotten, overlooked.

Toledo came to resemble some aging attempted suicide, bandaged up or scarred over. Attempts. Failures.

His memory phased out somewhere below the red seal on the label. He'd been talking to himself. Thoughts as little snatches of lyrical epiphany interspersed with dashes into the notebook. When he rolled out of the bed that morning to make the first pot of coffee he was genuinely relieved to find the notebook sitting on the floor beside his pants.

-

I just need it. I do. Lost.

-

The words were surprisingly legible for how messed up he must've been at that point in the evening. Little glimpses of a train lumbering by in the deepening dusk, a doe leaping off into the overgrowth, coupled with a hole the size of the sun in his heart. He remembered weeping. Really weeping. There. Alone. Sitting on an unused railroad tie, his head in his hands, his back quaking with a force he was sure was going to kill him then and there.

Then it passed.

Settled back down, the cat curling up by the

window for another heavy winter storm. Waiting. Tail swishing. He got up and—must've—finished the bottle.

"I guess I am. Lost."

He forced down the coffee and got ready for work.

-

"Here's your latte, sir."

"Hey, hey."

He turned back around to the counter.

"This isn't what I ordered."

"Oh."

"Jesus. Were you even listening? I repeated myself like three times. Are you stoned?"

"No, sir. Sorry. Let me remake it."

He took the cup from the man. There was such anger there. Disgust.

"What was it that you ordered, sir?"

"Are you fucking kidding me? I just told you. Where's your manager."

-

The first swallows brought tears to his eyes which stung in the crippling cold. He paused, gulped in the November night and drank more. He finished the bottle outside the store and walked back in and got another.

The tracks. The tracks, the tracks, the tracks, the tracks.

Where do they go? Where don't they go? Why don't you just take me somewhere?

Where can I go?

He worked on the bottle. He sang the little snatches to himself and, dutifully, scribbled a sentence down here and there.

He didn't know where he was. He'd set off without any sense of direction. He didn't recognize the backs of any of the buildings or houses that lined the tracks, so he just kept right on walking. He figured he'd get somewhere.

\-

What'll it be that saves me? Will it be a girl? A job? A purpose? How will I know it when it arrives?

I don't think the clouds part. I don't think there are trumpets. I don't believe that greeting card shit about "just knowing." I don't know shit.

Shit.

What if there isn't anything? That can save me? What if there is only the hourglass, dirty grains of sand, dropping like stones in a pond, until it's over?

\-

He'd made it home again. The afternoon sun was streaking in gray through the open bedroom window. A breeze ruffled the ragged curtains, second hand curtains. Goodwill curtains.

He looked at the clock. He was already late. He felt his stomach drop, knowing this was the end of this job. One in a long succession of lost jobs. A heaping pile of dead dead-end jobs.

He rolled over and went back to sleep.

\-

What is the defining moment? Where is the mover's hand? Where is the underlying current? The reason? The purpose?

\-

He ripped that page out and tossed it into the trash.

\-

He took the last of the money out of the bank. He bought a bottle. He walked the tracks.

"Rent's already late."

Sip.

"No more money coming in."

Sip.

His steps crunched in the gravel between ties. His boots were old, the soles barely holding together, and they squeaked a second before his foot hit the ground each time. It became the melody.

Where do you run when the nothing stretches out forever? Where do you go when you're at the bottom of the world?

He wished he had another bottle. He wished he had another home. Another job. Another life. He wished and wished and walked.

Night came and settled in. He lost feeling in his feet but kept them moving. He thought about freezing to death. Did he have the dignity to go quietly in the night, somewhere off the path, out of the way? Or would he lose his resolve and rush out into traffic waving his dick around to get arrested and out of the cold?

-

The darkness is blinding. It is its own light. The light of a thousand black suns more piercing than love.

-

There were drops of what he knew must be tears on the page. The writing wasn't slanted but obviously slowly, carefully written. The words had been important. The meaning stretched out between them like lifetimes.

"One's too many."

He would become that disheveled man in tattered clothing that talks to himself. Little bits of the interior dialogue bubbling up to the surface for the sane, rational world to balk at, laugh at.

This is the beginning of the end.

It felt like a song he'd been waiting to sing his

entire life.

-

When the levee breaks.

-

That was all the words he'd written for the past three days. He didn't know what city he was in any longer. Wasn't sure it was still Toledo or if he'd moved into Michigan or headed towards middle Ohio.

"Doesn't really matter, now does it?"

He guessed it didn't. Movement was about the only thing that mattered. Motion was his religion. The great shuffling of the feet. The blending of the landscape. The eternal directionlessness.

"The great distance."

But what was distance? How could it really be measured? Inches, feet, yards, miles? What were these constructs now? They were illusions. They were words. Words and words and words. The world is filled with them. His head felt sagging with them; overripened fruit blackened and sliming on the branch. The steps helped clear them. Not a lot but a little and that was better than nothing. There was too much nothing in the world already.

-

Found a box of raisins. They were mostly ok.

-

He pondered this entry for hours. There was a sage -like quality to it. Some unspoken truth hiding in there, maybe in the white spaces. Some old, asiatic monk robed with glittering eyes painting the words with the blackest ink. The haiku of honesty. The truest words the man had found.

"They were mostly ok," he repeated to himself again. "Mostly. Ok."

Somewhere along the way he'd picked up a cough. A hoarse, rattling thing that shook his chest like a cheap chandelier. It slowed him down.

His religion felt persecuted.

"This is my great hurdle."

He smiled to himself at the floating image of himself as a Puritan fleeing England. The first struggles of the burgeoning faith of motion. The first trial is stagnancy.

But hadn't that been the problem all along? he wondered.

Would they see him for what he was? The first martyr of the true religion?

He saw himself, shriveled up, purple and smiling, dead on the side the tracks. A police officer and an EMT standing there, little puffs of breath swirling from their noses in the early morning cold, discussing what they see as the passing of yet another drifter in the long winter night. Another nameless, meaningless person, lost and floating in an ever expanding, interconnected world.

"How do they get like this?" the EMT will ask.

"Dunno," the cop will say. "Choose it, I guess."

They'll nod their heads in unison and bag him up. His body, frozen with cold and the natural decay of life, will seem unseemly to them. His smile out of place.

Lewd.

Vulgar.

Like all things religious seen for the first time by the uninitiated. But that smile will make them neophytes. They'll go home at the end of their shifts and find their houses not quite as comfortable as they'd left them that morning. Their bellies not quite as full as they'd expected after what should've been a fully satisfying meal. Their beds will not cradle them into the peaceful sleep they'd grown so accustomed to.

"Martyr."

The word rang true. A crystalline bell pealing off into the nothing, encapsulating the piercing echo of lost humanity. The rock skipping out in front of his boots, clanging against the metal tracks, rang true. The shot in the dark that briefly illuminated the pale, shaking hands before the wide, craven eyes. The ravens grating in the ravine rang true. The echoes of honesty carried off with the stiff, cutting wind. He missed a step, stumbled, nearly fell and knew this, too, rang true.

A Truly Ugly River

Rivers can take you anywhere. That's what I used to think, staring down into the swirling, muddy water of the Ohio. It's a truly ugly river, the Ohio. An ugly state, too, but I digress. I used to sit for hours on this bench just across the river, the state line separating Indiana from Kentucky. With a book in my lap, unread, and my glasses reflecting off the hung sun, I watched.

I thought I wanted to run out and jump in. Just wade on out until I couldn't touch the bottom anymore and let it take me. All Virginia Woolfish, I know. But, at the time, it made perfect sense to me. Ashes to ashes, and all that. Because, you see, I was crying a lot back then. I still don't know where the half of it came from, the tears. They just poured forth like some broken down dam.

It didn't matter where I was either. Work, home, the grocery store, the pharmacy—picking up all the anti-depressants and antianxiety medicines that were flung at me by the bagful, none of which worked—it really didn't seem to matter.

No trigger warnings. Nothing really to set it off. Just life. And death and the constant thought that the two were really just different sides of the same coin. I was like that then. The always emotional naval-gazer. I couldn't see passed my own mortality and the time-stamp attached thereto.

Except when it came to the river.

It ran by with a consistency that was comforting. It called out to me: Look! I'm still here. Made of millions or billions or trillions of different water molecules—probably a corpse or two—but still here, still flowing, still moving on along to someplace else.

So, I'd go out there and sit. I'd walk there in the mornings on my days off or stumble down there after getting completely shit-faced at some redneck, soulless downtown bar.

Each drop, an escape. Each swirl, a beaconing.

I mean what else do you do when life has lost all meaning? Or maybe you've just discovered that it never had any to begin with?

You go and sit by the river and think about death and the constant rush of the shit-brown water. At least, that's what I did. And I'm still here, for now anyway. I mean, don't get me wrong, I haven't made any plans. I haven't made any plans to not have any plans either, though. So, there's that, too.

Anyway, one late September afternoon, sitting there on my bench by the river, the Ohio, with an immense Robert Jordan novel sitting unopened in my lap, it happened.

Flash.

Just like that, something was there. Some sense of self. All these, like, feelings came rushing up, from God knows where, and I thought I'd burst from all the pressure. I couldn't just sit there anymore. I had to move.

And there was the utter face of motion, right there, before me. It'd rained the past several days and the thing, the Ohio, was up, out of its banks like some foraging bear in a farmyard. Just poking its nose around, seeing what smells good, seeing what was left unattended to, you know, what was available.

I was available.

I let the book, borrowed from the library just that afternoon, drop onto the patchy grass and stood. At that moment, I knew exactly what it was to be the moth in the night seeing the glorious light shining so bright, so beautifully into the stillness of the dark. I felt the strings that are always there, hooks waiting for just the hint of motion, and I pulled. I wanted the hook.

It came. I felt it and knew that there are some hooks that are soft, more lulling than stabbing, but piercing just the same.

I walked across the small greenery to the thick, blocky rocks and stared down at the lapping water. The line was taut, I could feel it. It could snap at any moment. Whoever was on the other end had to play it safe, give me a little space.

Let the fish tucker itself out, my dad would say. Let it run a little.

I stood there, swaying and suddenly sweat drenched. This metallic bite wouldn't leave my throat, coating it in what I was sure would be rust-eaten silver if feelings could color. The immensity of the moment, the sheer knowledge that a step and a sucking in of several hundred water molecules would end it rocked me from my toes to my heels.

Have you ever wanted to feel absolutely nothing? I have. I do still, sometimes.

At that moment, I wanted nothing more. I wanted nothing.

My stomach, squeezed sharply in on itself, my

neck, strained, veins bulging, and my hands, curled into tight, little fists quaked. I shook. I thought, for a second, the earth, the rocks under my feet, the Ohio before me, the universe itself, shook right along with me.

Then the sharp sprinkle of a child's laughter.

That's what brought me back.

Some six-year old was throwing his legs behind him on the swing for all he was worth. I turned around and watched him, feeling a little testing tug at the line at my back. His eyes were squeezed shut, his head rocking on his little neck, swinging his legs forward on the out-shoot, tucking 'em tightly under on the swaying back.

His face was pure elation. The joy of motion. Of laughter. Of life. Of all the things ahead and behind, to the left and to the right, center and back, up and down.

I stepped away from the rocks, walked back to my borrowed book and the bench that suddenly appeared foreign to me, not caring that the tears were streaming down my face. That my stomach and chest shivered as if I were naked in January snows.

I scooped up my book and went out searching for that same joy.

artist picture courtesy of Adrian Lime

A.S. Coomer is a writer, musician, and artist. Books include: *Rush's Deal*, *The Fetishists*, *Shining the Light*, *Flirting with Disaster* & Other Poems, *The Devil's Gospel*, and *Memorabilia*. He runs Lost, Long Gone, Forgotten Records, a "record label" for poetry. He co-edits Cocklebur Press. www.ascoomer.com

www.ingramcontent.com/pod-product-compliance
Lightning Source LLC
Chambersburg PA
CBHW071952190726
48293CB00004B/1450